Jigger's Day Off

Michael Morpurgo
and Shoo Rayner

First published in Great Britain by
A & C Black (Publishers) Ltd 1990
First published by Collins 1990
9 8 7 6 5

Collins is an imprint of HarperCollins Children's Books part of
HarperCollins Publishers Ltd. 77-85 Fulham Palace Road, London W6 8JB

Text copyright © 1990 Michael Morpurgo
Illustrations copyright © 1990 Shoo Rayner. All rights reserved.

ISBN 0-00-673883 4

Printed and bound in Great Britain by
Caledonian International Book Manufacturing Ltd, Glasgow G64

Chapter One

There was once a family of all sorts of animals that lived in the farmyard behind the tumbledown barn down on Mudpuddle Farm.

Cocka-doodle-dooooo

At first light every morning, Frederick the flame-feathered cockerel lifted his eye to the sun and crowed and crowed . . .

until the light came on in old Farmer Rafferty's bedroom window.

3

One by one the animals crept out
into the dawn and stretched and
yawned and scratched themselves;
but no one ever spoke a word, not
until after breakfast.

You've got to get up,
you've got to get up,
you've got to get up
in the morning!
That Frederick sure can play the HORN!

'Jigger my dear,' said old Farmer Rafferty, one hazy hot morning in September.

And off he went.

'One day off a year,' thought Jigger, the always sensible sheepdog. 'One day a year when I don't have to be sensible, when I can do what a dog likes to do.' And he licked his smiling lips, and wagged his dusty tail.

Old Thunder lived all by himself in a shed at the end of the yard. No one ever went near him because no one dared.

Pintsize had never seen Old Thunder. He longed to peek in through the crack in the doors.

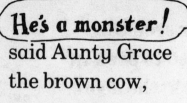

He's a monster!
said Aunty Grace
the brown cow,

I agree.

and of course
Primrose agreed
with her as she
always did.

Matter of fact, most of the animals
thought Old Thunder was some sort
of monster.

So when old Farmer Rafferty opened the door of the shed that morning, all the animals went into hiding. Upside and Down turned upside down in terror. Mossop disappeared into a drainpipe. (Everyone was terrified of Old Thunder – except Egbert the greedy goat. He was always too hungry to be frightened.)

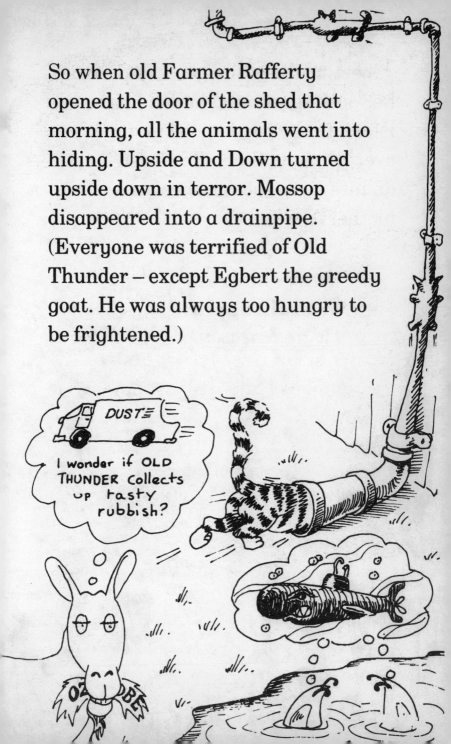

I wonder if OLD THUNDER collects up tasty rubbish?

Albertine the white goose gathered her goslings around her on her island in the pond and explained everything to them. She wasn't just an intelligent goose, she was a wise mother as well.

At that very and same moment,
there was a roar from inside Old
Thunder's shed, and he rumbled out
into the yard belching smoke and
dust. Old Farmer Rafferty sat high
and happy on the driver's seat
singing his heart out.

'See, children,' said Albertine gently. 'I told you that's all Old Thunder is, just an old combine harvester.'

Without him there'd be no straw to lie on in the winter and no corn to eat. Sometimes, children, I'm quite ashamed of my friends. I've told them and I've told them that Old Thunder only eats corn, but they just do not believe me.

One man went

Chapter Two

Old Thunder sailed majestically out through the gate and into the corn field beyond, his great cutters turning like the wheels of a giant paddle steamer. 'One man went to mow, went to mow a meadow,' sang old Farmer Rafferty in his crusty, croaky kind of voice.

to MOW. went to MOW a M

went

And behind him, Ji usually sensible sh through the gate ar the cut corn, his nos ground in between his paws.

SNIFF

W
Th
the
hidin
the ga
had fal

He smelt something,

SNIFF

and what he smelt

SNIFF

pleased him.

...ith the gate safely shut and Old
...under roaring round the field,
...animals at last crept out of their
...g places and stood watching by
...te – all except Mossop who
...en asleep in his drain.

ZZZZzz

'What's Jigger up to?' asked Diana the silly sheep, who always asked questions but never knew any answers.

Round and round the field went old
Thunder, churning out the straw
behind him in long and golden rows.
Round and round the field went
Jigger, slinking low to the ground.

And every now and then he would
stop and stare at the square of
standing corn, and every time
he stopped, the square was a little
bit smaller.

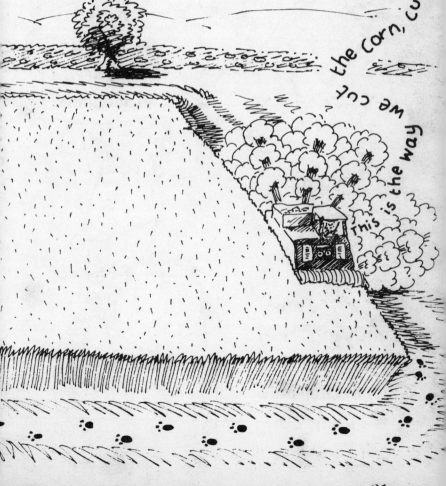

the corn, cut the cor

This is the way we cut

'We shouldn't be standing around in the sunshine,' said Captain.

Best go inside. those flies'll be at us soon.

So they did. Except for Egbert the goat who was busy chewing off the paint from the iron-barred gate.

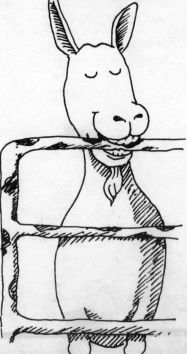

At eleven o'clock Old Thunder

stopped,

shuddered,

coughed

and was silent. The birds sang once more in the hedgerows.

Ever so carefully, for he was stiff in his knees, old Farmer Rafferty climbed down from his seat and sat down to rest in the shade.

It was time for his morning milk.
He *always* had it at eleven o'clock
no matter where, no matter what.

'I'm making sure old Thunder
doesn't miss anything,' said Jigger,
but he never took his eyes off the
standing corn.

And old Farmer Rafferty laughed
because he knew better.

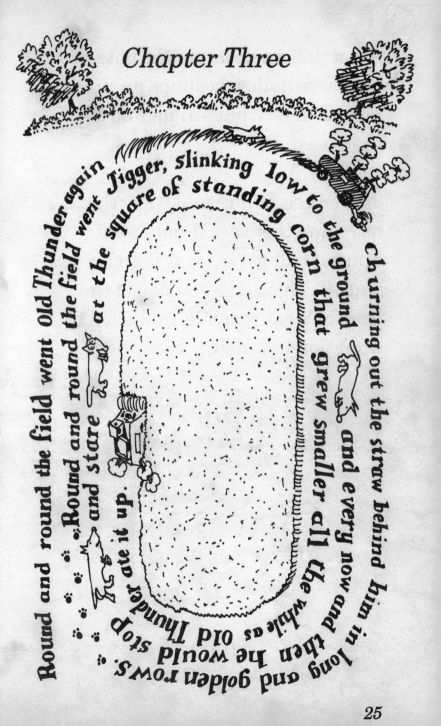

Chapter Three

Round and round the field went Old Thunder again, Round and round the field went Jigger, slinking low to the ground, churning out the straw behind him in long and golden rows. Round and round the field went smaller all the while as Old Thunder ate it up. And every now and then he would stop and stare at the square of standing corn that grew smaller all the while as Old Thunder ate it up.

Albertine was passing the gate with her three yellow goslings peeping behind her. 'What's Jigger up to?' they peeped.

'Never you mind,' said Albertine, hurrying them on. 'Jigger's not himself today, he never is on his day off. This is the one day of the year he's not sensible, and I don't want you to watch.'

I think he's Jiggered.

'Only mad dogs go out in the mid-day sun,' grumbled Egbert the goat, who had finished eating the paint on the gate.

'Mad dogs and goats,' said Albertine, but quietly so that Egbert would not hear. She never liked to upset anyone.

I like a bit of lead free paint!

27

At one o'clock old Thunder stopped again, shuddered, coughed and was silent. The birds sang once more in the hedgerows.

Ever so carefully, old Farmer Rafferty climbed down from his seat and sat down to eat his lunch in the shade – pasties and pickles.

He offered some to Jigger for he knew Jigger was partial to pasties. But Jigger was not interested in pasties – not today – he had his eye on the golden square of standing corn.

No thanks, can't stop for lunch.

Round and round the field went
Old Thunder again

churning out the straw behind him

in long and golden rows.

Round and round the field

went Jigger, slinking low

to the ground.

Captain plodded slowly down to the pond for a drink. 'Egbert,' he said, 'is Jigger still out there in this heat?'

'Must be mad, that dog,' said Egbert. 'Hasn't stopped all day. Round and round and round he goes – makes you dizzy just to look at him. Dunno why he bothers – he never catches anything.'

At four o'clock Old Thunder stopped again, shuddered, coughed and was silent. The birds sang once more in the hedgerows. Ever so carefully old Farmer Rafferty climbed down from his seat and walked off back towards the farmhouse to fetch his tea.

'Not much more to do,' he said as he went. 'Got 'em well and truly bottled up, have you, my dear? You'll never get 'em, Jigger, you never do.'

But Jigger was not listening to old Farmer Rafferty. He lay with his chin on his paws, his ears pricked forward towards the corn, his nose twitching.

Rabbits and hares, his nose told him,
rats and mice, moles and voles,
pheasants and partridges, beetles
and bugs.

He could hear them all rustling and
bustling and squeaking and
squealing in the little golden square
of standing corn that was left.

Sooner or later he knew they would
have to make a run for it.

Worry

Quake

Shivvver

And he'd be waiting.

Chapter Four

Jigger my dear!

It was old Farmer
Rafferty calling
from the house and
whistling for him.

'Jigger! Come boy, come boy! I know
it's your day off, but the sheep have
broken out in Back Meadow.
Come boy, come boy!'

I won't!
It's my one day off.
I'll be jiggered
if I'll go!

'Jigger! Jigger!' Old Farmer Rafferty
was using his nasty, raspy voice.

You come here
Jigger, else there'll
be trouble.

If I go now I'll
have wasted my
whole day. There'll
be nothing left
in that corn for
me to chase
when I get back.

And then he had an idea.

WOOF!
BARK!

Jigger's barking brought all the
animals running,

waddling

and flying
to the gate.

'Bring 'em all out into the field,
Captain,' he called out. The animals
all looked at each other nervously.

Don't worry
Old Thunder's
fast asleep.
He's been
working hard.

And so they all went out into the field, all except Diana the silly sheep who refused to go anywhere near old Thunder, whether he was asleep or not. Jigger quickly explained everything to Captain. And he went off towards the farmhouse.

WOOSH

In no time at all, Captain had them all organised and ready.

Nothing must leave the standing corn. Jigger says that we're to chase it back if anything comes out.

41

So Peggoty and
her little pigs,

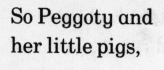

were sent to guard the north side of
the golden square of standing corn
along with Egbert.

Primrose and Aunty Grace went off to guard the south side with Albertine and her goslings.

Captain himself stayed to guard the east side with Frederick the cockerel.

And Mossop,
the cat with
the one and
single eye
was sent off
to guard the
west side.

So on three sides of the golden
square of standing corn the animals
kept watch.

But for Mossop it was
all too much. The sun was hot

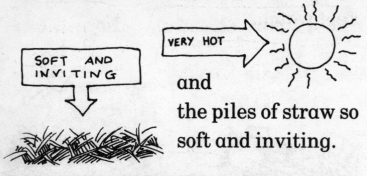

VERY HOT

SOFT AND INVITING

and
the piles of straw so
soft and inviting.

He lay down,

closed his
one

and single
eye

and

quite forgot what he was there for.

Chapter Five

Mossop snored as he slept, and
inside the golden square of corn
they heard him and saw him
and took their chance.

One by one the little creatures of the cornfield left their hiding places. In one long line they left – westwards . . .

Tee hee!

Rabbits first, then mice and

They tiptoed past the snoring cat
and out across the open field until
they reached the safety of the
hedgerow, where they vanished.

Chapter Six

Not long after this Jigger came haring back through the gate.

Didn't let anything escape, did you?

Not a one. Proper job we did for you Jigger, proper job.

And all the animals hurried back to the farmyard just in case Old Thunder woke up again – all of them except Mossop who still lay fast asleep in a pile of straw.

'Just this last little square to finish, Jigger,' said old Farmer Rafferty after he had finished his tea. 'Be finished by sundown, in spite of those darned sheep.'

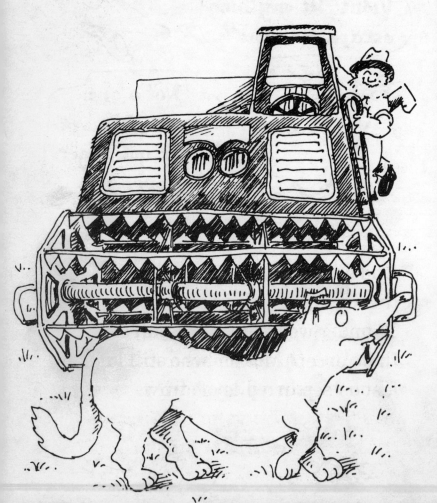

But Jigger was not listening. He
had other things on his mind. As Old
Thunder started up again he was
ready and waiting for the first of
the little creatures to break out of
their hiding place.

Round and round the field went Old Thunder for the last time, slinking low to the ground.

Round and round the field went Jigger for the last time, and Round the Field

54

time churning out straw behind him in long and golden rows. Round

By the time the sun set behind the tumble-down barn, not a stalk of corn was left standing. And nothing had come out, no rabbit, no rat, no mouse, no vole, no mole, no pheasant, no partridge, no beetle and no bug.

Nothing.

'Well I'll be jiggered,' said Jigger.

'It's the sun, Jigger,' said Mossop, who had just woken up. 'Does strange things to you.'

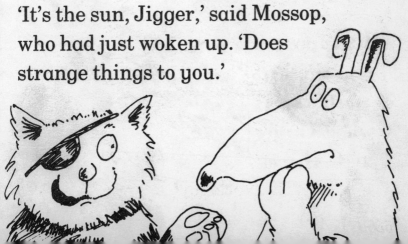

Too much Sun and you Can see things that aren't there,

So I suppose you can hear things and they're not there.

I suppose you can even smell things when they're not there.

I can tell you Jigger nothing came past me when I was on guard. Well they wouldn't dare, would they?

And he yawned hugely as cats do.

Jigger looked at Mossop sideways and wondered.

'Had a good day off, Jigger my dear?' old Farmer Rafferty shouted as he passed by high up on Old Thunder.

And old Farmer Rafferty laughed and laughed, until the laughter turned into a song once again.

One man and his dog, (woof! woof!) went to m
It's been a long day. Don't know about you, Jigger, but I'm just about ready for bed.
Tee hee!

And the night came down and the moon came up and everyone slept on Mudpuddle Farm.